Sleep-Over Mouse

Note

Once a reader can recognize and identify the 32 words used to tell this story, he or she will be able to read successfully the entire book. These 32 words are repeated throughout the story, so that young readers will be able to easily recognize the words and understand their meaning.

The 32 words used in this book are:

a	he's	over	tents
and	is	play	there
anyone's	little	plenty	to
at	loves	share	too
can	make	sheets	toys
do	meet	sleep	treats
fun	mouse	sleep-over	with
he	noise	Squeak	you

Library of Congress Cataloging-in-Publication Data
Packard, Mary.
    Sleep-over mouse/by Mary Packard : illustrated by Kathy Wilburn.
        p.   cm. — (My first readers)
    Summary: Squeak is a little mouse who loves to sleep over at
anyone's house.
        ISBN 0-516-05367-1
        (1. Sleepovers—Fiction. 2. Mice—Fiction. 3. Stories in rhyme.)
        I. Wilburn, Kathy, ill. II. Title.
III. Series: My first reader.
PZ8.3.P125S1 1994
(E)—dc20   94-16943
                                                CIP
                                                AC

Sleep-Over Mouse

Written by Mary Packard   Illustrated by Kathy Wilburn

CHILDREN'S PRESS
A Division of Grolier Publishing
Sherman Turnpike
Danbury, Connecticut 06816

Meet little Squeak.

He's a sleep-over mouse.

Squeak loves to sleep over

at anyone's house.

He loves to share toys.

He loves to share treats.

He loves to make noise,

and make tents with sheets.

A sleep over is fun.

There is plenty to do!

Squeak loves to play.

He loves to sleep, too.

Can sleep-over mouse

sleep over with you?

MAIL

ABOUT THE AUTHOR

Mary Packard is the author of more than 150 books for children. Packard lives in Northport, New York, with her husband and two daughters. Besides writing, she loves music, theater, walks on the beach, animals, and, of course, children of all ages.

ABOUT THE ILLUSTRATOR

Kathy Wilburn grew up in Kansas City, Missouri, and began her artistic career there, with Hallmark Cards. Now, she lives in Portland, Oregon, where she works as a children's book illustrator and writer. Wilburn has two sons, Christopher and Randy, who are students of art and music. She loves nature, cats, blues music, and beautiful old cars.